Popsicle Polly

by Katherine Alyssa Sherman

Illustrated by Inji Kang

Book illustrations by Inji Kang

ISBN 979-8-9859598-2-6

To my mom, my aunt, and Inji,

Thank you for all your hard work to help make my life-long dream come true.
It's been a long journey, and it couldn't have happened without you all.

Once upon a time,

there was

a little girl

named

Polly.

Polly loved to eat

popsicles.

She would eat them for breakfast,

lunch,

AND

dinner!

Every day
when Polly went to school,
her mom would pack
her lunch with veggies.

Polly did not like
healthy veggies!

She thought

they were icky

because

they looked

green and mushy.

All Polly liked were popsicles.

So, every day
she would sneak one
into her lunch box.

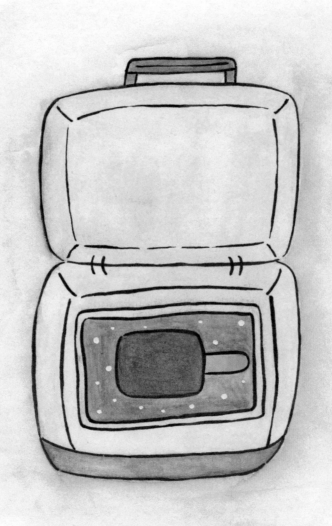

During lunch,

Polly would ignore

her veggies

and

only eat

her popsicle.

One evening during dinner time,
Polly's mom told her,
"No more popsicles,"

and this made Polly very mad.

She threw
all her veggies
on the floor

and ran to her room.

Polly's mom called out after her saying,
"If you keep
eating popsicles, one day,
you're going to
turn into one!"

The next day,
Polly was still very upset.

Before her mom took her to school,

Polly snuck TWO popsicles
into her lunch box.

At school, it was
lunch time for Polly,

and just like always,

she ignored

her veggies

and only ate

her popsicles.

But this time

something went wrong!

Polly started to feel cold.

Very cold.

She looked down at her feet,
and they were frozen!

Soon her legs were frozen too!

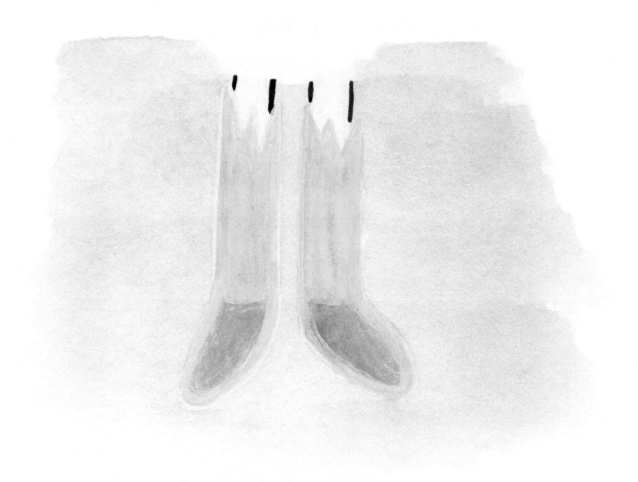

Before long,
Polly was frozen
up to her waist.

Her whole body
was turning into ice!

Her teacher was scared, so
she called Polly's mom.

"Hi. This is Polly's teacher. Something is happening to Polly!

You need to come quick!"

So, Polly's mom
rushed over to the school

to find her daughter
FROZEN in ice
up to her head!

While the teacher
and other students
were scared, Polly's mom
knew just what to do.

She reached into Polly's lunch box
and grabbed a steaming hot piece of
broccoli packed this morning.

Polly's mom put the broccoli
into Polly's mouth and
told her to eat it.

As Polly began to chew,
the ice began to melt.

The warmth of the broccoli
was melting the ice away!

So, Polly kept eating and her mom kept feeding her veggies until the ice was all gone!

As she gobbled them up,
Polly realized that veggies were
a good thing!

Then,
Polly's mom took her home
and that night
for dinner,

Polly asked for a huge plate
of veggies!

So, remember to eat
your veggies or

you might just turn into a popsicle!

Made in the USA
Coppell, TX
27 July 2023

19665823R00031